A NOTE TO PARENTS

Reading is one of the most important gifts we can give our children. How can you help your child to become interested in reading? By reading aloud!

My First Games Readers make excellent read-alouds and are the very first books your child will be able to read by him/herself. Based on the games children know and love, the goals of these books include helping your child:

- **learn sight words**
- **understand that print corresponds to speech**
- **understand that words are read from left to right and top to bottom**

Here are some tips on how to read together and how to enjoy the fun activities in the back of these books:

Reading Together

- Set aside a special time each day to read to your child. Encourage your child to comment on the story or pictures or predict what might happen next.
- After reading the book, you might wish to start lists of words that begin with a specific letter (such as the first letter of your child's name) or words your child would like to learn.
- Ask your child to read these books on his/her own. Have your child read to you while you are preparing dinner or driving to the grocery store.

Reading Activities

- The activities listed in the back of this book are designed to use and expand what children know through reading and writing. You may choose to do one activity a night, following each reading of the book.
- Keep the activities gamelike and don't forget to praise your child's efforts!

Whatever you do, have fun with this book as you pass along the joy of reading to your child. It's a gift that will last a lifetime!

Wiley Blevins, Reading Specialist
Ed.M. Harvard University

ISBN 0-439-26465-0

12 11 10 9 8 7 6 5 4 3 2 1   1 2 3 4 5 6/0

Illustrated by Guy Francis
Designed by Peter Koblish

Printed in the U.S.A.
First Scholastic printing, April 2001

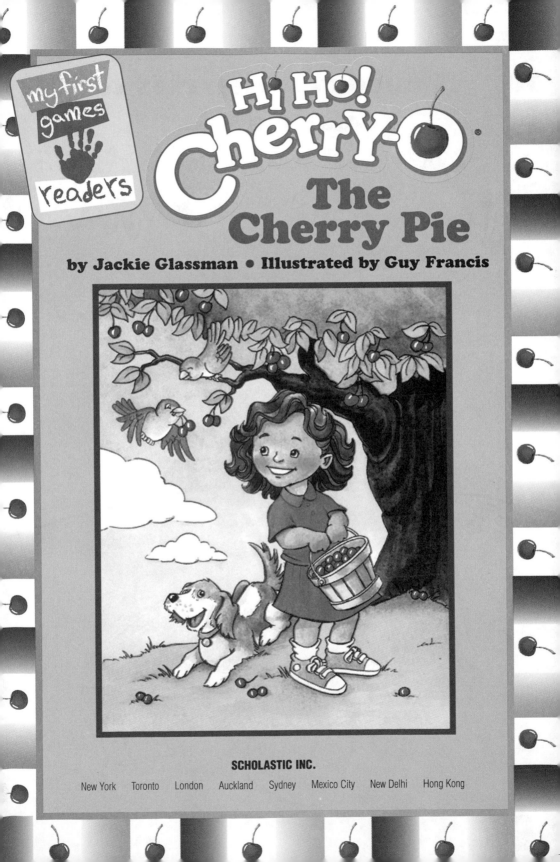

Hi Ho! Cherry-O
The Cherry Pie

by Jackie Glassman • Illustrated by Guy Francis

SCHOLASTIC INC.

New York   Toronto   London   Auckland   Sydney   Mexico City   New Delhi   Hong Kong

I need ten cherries to make a pie.

I pick a cherry off a tree.
I pick two more.

That makes three.

Picking cherries is lots of fun.
My basket falls.

Now I have none!

I climb a tree to pick some more.
Oh, look! Oh, look!

I see four.

Here is my best friend, Evan.
He has three cherries.

We have seven!

The dog is chasing after sticks.
He eats one cherry.

I am down to six.

My pal Kate is really great.
She finds two cherries.

Now we have eight.

Two big birds fly up to me.
They eat five cherries!

Yikes! I have just three.

I climb the tree for
one more try.

I find seven cherries.
Now we can have pie!

Yummy!

Ch Is For . . .
Which of these begins with "ch"?

Cherry Pattern

On a separate piece of paper, finish the cherry pattern.

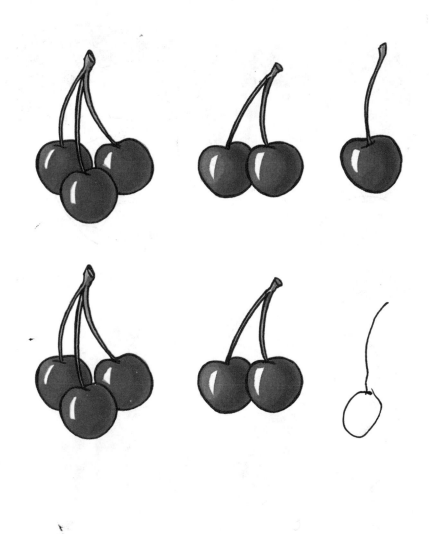

Crazy Upside-down Day

What's wrong with this picture? Write down everything you find on a separate sheet of paper.

Rhyme Lines

I see a <u>pie</u> in the <u>sky</u> .

I see a <u>bee</u> with a <u>tree</u>.

I see a <u>cat</u> in the <u>Hat</u> .

A Basket of Cherries

In the story, the number of cherries in the basket keeps changing. Put the baskets of cherries in the same order as they appear in the story.

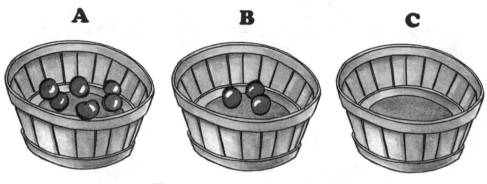

A   B   C

D   E

F   G   H

About Face!

Here are pictures of the kids from the story. Look at their faces and tell what you think they are feeling.

Hungry Animals

In the story, the dog and two birds eat some of the cherries. On a separate sheet of paper, draw a picture of another animal eating cherries. Write the number of cherries the animal is eating.

Cherry Math

Use a separate sheet of paper to draw an answer to each picture problem.

1. **1 cherry + 2 cherries =** 3

2. **4 cherries + 3 cherries =** 7

3. **3 cherries – 2 cherries =** 1

4. **5 cherries – 1 cherry =** 4

Answers

Cherry Math

1. 3 cherries
2. 7 cherries
3. 1 cherry
4. 4 cherries

Cherry Pattern

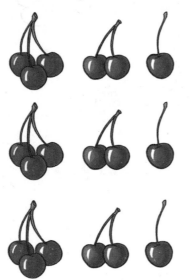

Rhyme Lines

I see a PIE in the SKY.

I see a BEE with a TREE.

I see a CAT in the HAT.

"Ch" Is For . . .

These begin with "ch":

A Basket of Cherries

B or F, C, H, G, A, D,
F or B, E

Crazy Upside-down Day